JE
Wallace, Karen.   RED READER
Where are my shoes?

MID-CONTINENT PUBLIC LIBRARY
Lee's Summit Branch
150 NW Oldham Parkway
Lee's Summit, MO 64081

LS

WITHDRAWN
FROM THE RECORDS OF TH
MID-CONTINENT PUBLIC LIBR/

Where are my Shoes?

This edition first published in 2006 by
Sea-to-Sea Publications
1980 Lookout Drive
North Mankato
Minnesota 56003

Text © Karen Wallace 2003, 2006
Illustration © Deborah Allwright 2003

Printed in China

All rights reserved

Library of Congress Cataloging-in-Publication Data:

Wallace, Karen.
   Where are my shoes? / by Karen Wallace.
     p. cm. — (Reading corner)
   Summary: While searching for his shoes, Jack finds a magic wand, a cape, and a
   top hat.
   ISBN 1-59771-002-4
   [1. Lost and found possessions—Fiction. 2. Shoes—Fiction. 3. Magic—Fiction.] I. Title.
   II. Series.

PZ7.W1568Wh 2005
[E]—dc22

                                                              2004063633

9 8 7 6 5 4 3 2

Published by arrangement with the Watts Publishing Group Ltd, London

Series Editor: Jackie Hamley
Series Advisors: Linda Gambrell, Dr. Barrie Wade, Dr. Hilary Minns
Design: Peter Scoulding

To Glenn, from KW

Where are my Shoes?

Written by
Karen Wallace

Illustrated by
Deborah Allwright

SEA-TO-SEA
Mankato Collingwood London

MID-CONTINENT PUBLIC LIBRARY
Lee's Summit Branch
150 NW Oldham Parkway
Lee's Summit, MO 64081
LS

MID-CONTINENT PUBLIC LIBRARY - BTM

3 0003 00069536 9

Karen Wallace
"I love writing funny books so I can laugh at my own jokes. I wish I'd had a pair of shoes like Jack's when I was younger!"

Deborah Allwright
"I'm always working towards making my shoe collection even bigger!"

Jack is cross. "Where are my shoes?"

Are they under the bed?

8

No, but here is a wand!

Are they behind
the door?

11

No, but here is a cloak!

Are they on the table?

15

No, but here is a top hat!

"Where are your shoes?" shouts Mom.

19

Abracadabra!

"Here are my shoes!"
cries Jack.

Notes for parents and teachers

READING CORNER has been structured to provide maximum support for new readers. The stories may be used by adults for sharing with young children. Primarily, however, the stories are designed for newly independent readers, whether they are reading these books in bed at night, or in the reading corner at school or in the library.

Starting to read alone can be a daunting prospect. READING CORNER helps by providing visual support and repeating words and phrases, while making reading enjoyable. These books will develop confidence in the new reader, and encourage a love of reading that will last a lifetime!

If you are reading this book with a child, here are a few tips:

1. Make reading fun! Choose a time to read when you and the child are relaxed and have time to share the story.

2. Encourage children to reread the story, and to retell the story in their own words, using the illustrations to remind them what has happened.

3. Give praise! Remember that small mistakes need not always be corrected.

READING CORNER covers three grades of early reading ability, with three levels at each grade. Each level has a certain number of words per story, indicated by the number of bars on the spine of the book, to allow you to choose the right book for a young reader:

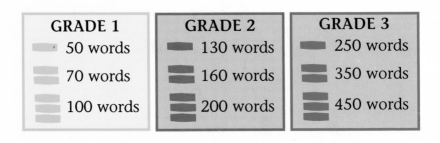

GRADE 1	GRADE 2	GRADE 3
50 words	130 words	250 words
70 words	160 words	350 words
100 words	200 words	450 words